G.H.O.S.T. SQUAD

PHANTOM at the FUNHOUSE

By Brittany Canasi

Illustrated by Katie Wood

Rourke
Educational Media
rourkeeducationalmedia.com

www.rourkeeducationalmedia.com

Edited by: Keli Sipperley
Cover layout by: Tara Raymo
Interior layout by: Kathy Walsh
Cover and Interior Illustrations by: Katie Wood

Library of Congress PCN Data

Phantom at the Funhouse / Brittany Canasi
 (G.H.O.S.T. Squad)
 ISBN 978-1-68342-343-0 (hard cover)(alk. paper)
 ISBN 978-1-68342-439-0 (soft cover)
 ISBN 978-1-68342-509-0 (e-Book)
 Library of Congress Control Number: 2017931187

Printed in the United States of America,
North Mankato, Minnesota

All cheer. No fear. That's the G.H.O.S.T Squad's motto. These girls hunting oddities and supernatural things are always up to something, whether it's cheerleading practice, pep rallies, or investigating spooks.

Mags, Scarlett, and Luna have built a business helping the haunted. And, along with Scarlett's service dog, Dakota, they're scaring up a lot of fun in the process. Each book in the G.H.O.S.T Squad series is self-contained, so they don't have to be read in any particular order. And every book is teeming with back matter, including an explainer section on paranormal studies, information about a real reportedly haunted location like that in the story, author interviews, and further reading suggestions.

Meet the Authors:
Brittany Canasi and K.A. Robertson have wanted to collaborate on a fiction series for years. And now they have! They worked together to develop the characters and concepts that drive the G.H.O.S.T Squad series, then they each wrote their books based on those ideas, helping each other shape their manuscripts along the way.

Meet the Illustrator:
Katie Woods' talent and commitment to bringing the G.H.O.S.T Squad characters to life were invaluable to the series. Katie is never happier than when she is drawing, and is living her dream as a freelance illustrator. She works happily from her studio in Leicester, England, and her work is published all over the world.

"The wonderful characters in this book have been an endless source of delight and inspiration. It has been so exciting to be part of the G.H.O.S.T Squad team and find out what adventures these girls will encounter next!" Katie says.

Brittany, K.A., Katie and the entire Rourke team hope these books tickle your funny bone and scare you silly!

Happy reading,
Rourke Educational Media

Meet the
G.H.O.S.T. Squad

*(Girls Hunting Oddities
& Supernatural Things)*

Luna: Discovered her psychic abilities in third grade, when a spirit warned her about the vegetables hidden under her pizza cheese. That night she also discovered her mother, a popular (and totally embarrassing) psychic on TV, is not psychic at all.

Other: Loves soccer and cheerleading. Hates broccoli.

Mags: Short for Magdeline. Her family has lived in New Orleans since it was founded in 1718. They know pretty much everything about everyone. And if they don't know, Mags knows how to dig up the dirt. Mags has a brain full of history knowledge and she's not afraid to use it.

Other: Best back tuck on the cheer squad. Afraid of clowns and pufferfish. (Don't ask why, she won't talk about it.)

Scarlett: Cheer captain, skeptic, and technology genius. Enjoys code cracking, hacking, and teaching her service dog, Dakota, strange tricks. Lost her lower leg in an accident. Became gymnast and cheerleader soon after.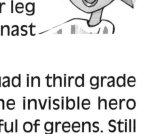

Other: Founded G.H.O.S.T. Squad in third grade after Luna told her about the invisible hero who saved her from a mouthful of greens. Still doesn't totally believe in ghosts. Still totally loves ghost hunting.

Dakota: Labrador. Scarlett's service dog. Recently learned to skateboard and sneeze on command. But not at the same time. Yet.

Other: Can smell ghosts. Will do anything for bacon.

Case ID: Freaky1

Location: Mirror Funhouse, Carnival at Sunshine Middle School

Background:
Rumors of a haunted funhouse leaves people not wanting to go to the carnival.

Reported Activity:

- Ghost-like figure appears in the funhouse behind glass.

Possible causes:

- Someone playing a sick joke.
- Evil math teacher scaring kids into going home and doing homework?
- Rumors. No one has actually seen a ghost.

Table of Contents

Chapter 1
CARNIVAL CHAOS

It wasn't even first period yet, and the G.H.O.S.T. Squad was sitting in the principal's office.

"What did we do this time?" Mags whispered to Luna and Scarlett. The three of them, and Scarlett's trusty service dog, Dakota, sat in a tight row on the bench in front of the principal's desk, while the head honcho herself was somewhere else. She was probably doing this on purpose to build up suspense.

Total power move.

"Did Scarlett hack the marquee in the front of the school again?" Luna asked.

"That was one time!" Scarlett said.

Luna and Mags both gave Scarlett a look that said, *Oh, come on!*

"What? Logan Williams made fun of my leg, so I thought someone should make fun of the fact that he peed his pants in gym that one time," she said, glancing down at her prosthetic leg.

"It may have been one time, but it was up for half the day before anyone figured it out,"

Luna said.

"I kind of think he deserved it," Mags said.

"Well, yeah. He definitely did. That's not

even an argument. But having Scarlett banned from cheer squad for a month and not having our best base was a bummer," Luna said.

"Worth it," Scarlett said with a wicked smile.

The door swung open with a flourish, and Principal Mabry hurried to her desk. She straightened her suit and sat.

"So sorry to keep you waiting, girls. Thank you for coming down to meet with me," she said.

"Did we have a choice?" Scarlett mumbled, earning an elbow from Mags.

"We have a problem," Principal Mabry said. "I have a haunted carnival, a school in bad need of repair, and not much time to find another fundraiser to get the money we need."

"Oh, this is a business meeting. I feel underdressed. I should've put on my fancy leg, Scarlett said."

She wiggled her prosthetic leg, earning a groan from Mags and Luna and a very awkward, confused stare from her principal.

"As I was saying, I know this is a bit unorthodox, asking a group of children to get rid of a ghost for me. But I'm a bit desperate, and word on the street is that you girls are good at what you do."

"What's in it for us?" Scarlett asked. Luna shoved her hand over Scarlett's mouth to keep her from saying another word.

"We'd love to help out in any way we can,

Principal Mabry," Luna said, giving Scarlett major side-eye.

Principal Mabry smiled sweetly at them, apparently way too polite to point out Scarlett's momentary verbal vomit. Which, if she knew Scarlett better, she'd know wasn't so momentary at all.

"It's reportedly coming from the funhouse. The one with the glass and mirrors. Kids are running out screaming, claiming to see a ghost. Parents don't seem to buy it, but kids are scared to come to the carnival. Attendance has dropped dramatically in just the first week. I'm afraid if things don't pick up and the fundraiser is a bust, it's going to look pretty bleak around these halls."

"We'll start investigating right away, Principal Mabry. You're in good hands with us."

"I knew I would be. And don't worry, I don't expect you girls to do this for nothing."

"Go on," Scarlett said. She leaned over, resting her elbows on her knees and her chin on her hands.

"How about the cheerleading squad gets first pick of the school buses for all away games this year?" Principal Mabry asked.

"You got yourself a deal," Scarlett said, holding her hand out to shake the principal's hand. Principal Mabry looked down at her hand for a moment before taking it in a quick shake, probably not used to striking business deals with students.

"All right, off I go. There's a spicy salsa-eating contest in the teacher's lounge in five minutes, and I'm the referee. See yourselves out, ladies," the principal said, leaving the room in a flurry.

"You know, it'd be worth the detention just to sneak in there and watch. I bet our science teacher would win, since I'm pretty sure he's a robot," Luna said.

"How is he a robot?" Scarlett asked as she stood up. Dakota stood at attention, ready to walk next to her owner and best buddy.

"He squeaks when he walks. His joints need some oil."

"Those are his shoes against the floor, you weirdo," Mags said.

"Don't challenge me. I know what I'm talking about," Luna said.

Chapter 2
NOT-SO-FUNHOUSE

 Squad

Mags:
head 2 carnival after practice?

Luna:
CAN'T :*(have to help Mom w/ show

Scarlett:
OK cool we'll use our other psychic friend 2 talk w the ghost

Luna:
wait u guys have another psychic friend????

Mags:
- _____- no, luna

Luna:
u guys r the worst

After cheer practice, Mags, Scarlett, and Dakota walked over to the baseball field, which had been temporarily repurposed as the carnival grounds.

"How are we supposed to do this without Luna?" Scarlett asked. "She's the one who actually can tell when they're there."

Mags dug through her backpack and pulled out her EMF meter.

"When we can't rely on Luna, we rely on electronics," she said with a smile.

Scarlett took the EMF meter from Mags and studied it. She'd used it plenty before, but it was always in conjunction with Luna being able to sense them, too. They almost never solely relied on their gear.

"Yeah, but Luna can tell when they're angry or sad or whatever. This thing just tells me a dead thing's near."

"Well, it'll have to do," Mags said.

The two of them, with Dakota in tow, walked into the funhouse. Even in the middle of the day, the place was spooky. Once they went through the entrance, there was little natural light coming in. And since it wasn't during operating hours, all the dim overhead lights were out, too.

Mags and Scarlett turned on their phone flashlights to take a look around. Every other surface was alternating from glass to mirror, all smudged with fingerprints.

"I'm not getting anything," Scarlett said, holding up the EMF meter.

"Let's walk further in," Mags said.

"It smells like someone spilled a bottle of window cleaner in here."

"It really does. Let's get this over with before it burns the inside of my nose and I never smell anything ever again," Mags said.

Scarlett sighed, flashing her phone's light ahead of them as they made their way through the glass-and-mirror maze. They stopped every few feet to check around them. They made it near the end with still no luck.

The EMF meter spiked, making a quick, high-pitched clicking sound.

"We got it! The ghost!" Scarlett whispered. Her head whipped from one side to another, trying to see something. But nothing was there.

"Do you feel anything? A breeze? Something cold?" Mags said. "I feel nothing."

Scarlett raised her arm to hold up her phone's light again, when she saw it:

She had just gotten a text message from her

mom.

"Oh, sorry. It was my phone that spiked the EMF. My mom wants me to grab milk on the way home."

"Fine. We might as well go. We've been here long enough, and it looks like the story was bogus. Let's get back," Mags said.

Scarlett nodded in the dark as she turned the EMF meter to the side to switch it off. But just as she touched the switch, it spiked again.

"Your mom must really want some dairy," Mags said.

But there were no new notifications on Scarlett's phone.

"Mags?" Scarlett whispered.

Dakota whimpered and backed up a few paces, her tail tucked firmly between her legs.

Scarlett and Mags locked hands and looked back at the same time.

Right behind Dakota, in a fingerprint-smudged window, was a the faint image of a man.

He looked old.

He looked mad.

And he most definitely didn't look alive.

Scarlett squeezed Mags' hand so tight she thought it might break.

"Don't scream. Just run," Mags said.

"Dakota, go!" Scarlett whispered as loud as she could. Dakota dutifully took off running, and the two girls followed after.

They ran all the way off the baseball field before they stopped. Mags rested her hands on her knees to catch her breath as Scarlett hugged her arms around herself.

"Do you ever wish you had a normal after-school gig? Like babysitting or washing cars or something?" Scarlett asked.

"Most of the time, no. But after that? I'd take on even the grossest diaper," Mags said.

Chapter 3
WHO KNOWS WHAT?

Investigation Updates:

Is definitely a ghost. Old man. Angry.

(Might still be an old man prankster)

No, it's definitely a ghost.

Yeah, okay fine. It's definitely a ghost.

"I'm telling you, Luna. This guy was terrifying. You could tell he was angry about something," Scarlett said.

The G.H.O.S.T. Squad was hanging out in Luna's bedroom that Friday night, trying to figure out just who the ghost could possibly be.

Dakota listened intently while she chewed on a bone near the foot of the bed.

"Do you see anything online about people dying at the carnival? I can't imagine a funhouse is all that dangerous," Luna said.

"Nothing. I've been checking into the carnival company's insurance claims. They have a pretty spotless record. No accidents reported other than the occasional kid falling off a ride for not wearing a seatbelt. Nothing more than a broken bone, though," Scarlett said.

"I can't believe your parents bought you a subscription to a super secret detective database for your birthday. I asked for a new bicycle," Mags said.

"I think next I'll look up Principal Mabry's address so I can TP her house as revenge for getting us mixed up with evil carnival dude," Scarlett said.

"Yeah, that'll be great for business," Luna mumbled.

"I think we're going to have to go about this the old-fashioned way," Mags said. "We need a ride to the carnival so we can do some digging. Ask the staff if they know anything."

"I'll ask my brother," Luna said, pulling out her phone.

Chapter 4
GHOST TALES

Luna:
need a ride. HELP PLZ.

Jeremy:
busy. ask Mom

Luna:
she's gonna talk about her fake
ghosts the whole time.

Jeremy:
sry. band practice in 15

"Your brother's room is right next to yours. Please tell me you're not texting him," said Mags.

"His room smells like gym socks. I avoid that place at all costs."

Scarlett and Mags twisted their faces in disgust, and Dakota shook her head and buried it under the bed.

"Probably best we don't ride with him anyway."

"Well, brace yourselves, then. We're about to hear another story from the Most Amazing Psychic Medium Ever!" Luna said, faking the enthusiasm of an announcer. "My mom will be taking us to the carnival."

"I'm telling you girls, you should have seen the place. Nail polish bottles broken. The whole place reeked of nail polish remover. It looked like the place had been hit by a tornado," Luna's mom said as she craned her neck toward the back of the car.

Luna already knew how this story went, seeing as she had to be there to help film it, on "a very special episode" of "The Most Amazing Psychic Medium Ever!" It was a nail salon that was haunted, and only her mother was able to expel the ghost.

What the viewers didn't know was that her mother paid her cousin $300 to use her nail salon after hours to fake the whole thing. And

while it sounded pretty crooked, her cousin could use the cash, and her mother's viewers got another half hour of entertainment. Seeing as most of them called with fake dead relatives for her to "contact," Luna was pretty sure everyone was in on the joke.

"How did you get rid of the ghost this time?" Mags said. Luna was impressed by how genuine she sounded.

"So glad you asked!" Luna's mom said cheerily. "We used sage. See, you burn it, wave it in the air like so," she said, waving one arm above her in slow motion. "The smoke from the sage banishes unwanted spirits. My client was able to get back to business after a little cleaning."

"That owner's really lucky to have your help," Mags said, earning a bright smile from Luna's mom.

Luna peered into the backseat to see the looks on her friends' faces. They both gave her a knowing smile, and Luna mouthed, *Thanks*. Her mom didn't know they knew the truth, and it was probably best to keep it like that.

Chapter 5
BILL SQUARED

No one at the carnival was saying a word.

The G.H.O.S.T. Squad spread out and asked every operator at every ride and every person manning games.

"The woman at the spinning space seemed like she knew something, but she just mumbled something about 'ghosts aren't real' and 'boss says we can't talk about it' and shooed me away," Mags said.

"That's better than the guy at the balloons and darts stand. He threatened to throw darts at me if I didn't go away. Rather prickly of him," Scarlett said.

"I'm guessing the pun was intended on that one," Luna said, giving Scarlett a suspicious look.

"Always. It's always intended," Scarlett said with a satisfied smile, earning groans from Luna and Mags.

"Well the only ride left is the Ferris wheel. Shall we?" Luna asked.

The girls nodded and walked over to the

ride. They waited for some riders to exit and climbed up the stairs of the exit to get closer to the operator.

"Line's around that way," the operator said, pointing without making eye contact.

"Sir, we just have a couple of questions for you. About the mirror funhouse and the disturbances that've been going on," Mags said in her most professional tone—her *#bosswoman* tone, according to Scarlett.

The operator grunted and continued letting kids on the ride, hitting the switch, and resting against the control panel in front of him.

"If we're able to figure out what's going on, we can probably fix it. That would mean more people would come to the carnival, and the carnival would make more money," Mags said, her voice hopeful.

"Good one," Luna whispered.

"Tell you what," the ride operator said, finally turning around. "As you can see, I've been pretty slow. You guys come stand in line, pay to get on the ride, and I'll tell you what I know."

"You got a deal," Scarlett yelled as she pulled Mags from the exit. They walked around to the line, which only had five people in it, and

waited their turn.

After only a few minutes, they made their way to the front of the line and stood eagerly at the chain dividing them from the operator.

"All right, first question," Scarlett said. "Has anyone ever died here?"

"You kids and your manners. You can't just ask if someone died in my place of work," the operator said, looping his thumbs in his suspenders.

"I can if we only have thirty seconds before I get stuck on this thing," Scarlett said, gesturing toward the Ferris wheel.

"Fine. Bill Williams," the guy said.

"Wait. His name was William Williams?" Luna asked.

"I ain't his parents. I didn't name him. He was a rotten old man anyway, almost got me fired once just because I got the flu and needed time off," the operator grumbled. He stopped the ride and opened the gate.

"Get on," he said, nodding toward the just-emptied car with the open door. "And hold on to the dog."

"But we have a few more questions!" Mags said.

"We had a deal, and I'm going on my break.

You can talk to Steve now," he said.

Steve stepped over the chain and walked over to the control panel, nodding at the other operator. Steve was about six and a half feet tall, probably over three hundred pounds, and had a crease in his brow that said he'd never had a good day in his life.

"Well?" Steve asked, looking at the girls and then the open door.

They jumped into the ride and shut the door behind them.

They would not be asking Steve any questions.

"Now what?" Luna asked.

"Now we look up Bill Williams and what happened to him. All I needed was a name," Scarlett said.

"Genius!" Mags said.

Chapter 6
GOTCHA!

Scarlett opened her messenger bag and pulled out the tablet they were all issued at school. The tablets were all on lockdown so they were mostly only able to use their e-textbooks, a couple of school-related apps, and basic research. But about an hour after receiving hers, Scarlett hacked it so she could use it for whatever she wanted.

"William Williams. Carnival," she said aloud as she typed. She bit the inside of her cheek as she anxiously waited for the search results.

"Got it! The Des Moines Monitor has an article. Must've been where it happened," she said, scooting closer to the other girls as she put a protective arm around Dakota. Dakota's tongue was hanging out, here eyes closed as the breeze from the moving ride hit her in the face. She was wearing the dog version of a huge, dopey smile.

The Des Moines Monitor
#1 rated online newspaper by people who rate online newspapers*

*not independently verified

Police Blotter
October 15

Police responded to reports of a body at the Sunny Day Elementary annual carnival. The man is believed to be William Williams, one of the attraction operators. He has no surviving family members, and judging by the nasty things said about him that morning, did not have any known friends.

Comments...

OldManBillsTheWorst99 (2 years ago)
> *This guy chased us out of the funhouse because we kept touching the glass. It's a carnival, man. Lighten up.*

ButImTheGreatest (2 years ago)
> *We were just there last week! This guy yelled at my 4 year old cousin for taking too long.*

PizzaFace (2 years ago)
> *Y is everyone complaining about a dead person?? The Internet is weird...*

OldManBillsTheWorst99 (2 years ago)
> *NO PIZZAFACE YOU'RE WEIRD*

"Sounds like Bill Williams was kind of awful," Mags said.

"Almost as awful as Internet comments," Scarlett grumbled.

Their Ferris wheel car approached the bottom of the ride, and Steve's stare drilled straight through them from the control panel. No, they definitely would not be speaking to Steve this evening.

"How are we getting rid of Old Man Bill?" Scarlett asked as they walked through the sparse crowd of carnival-goers.

"Oh, are we adopting an Internet commenter's name for him?" Mags asked.

"Whatever, it's catchy," Scarlett said, shrugging.

"I know!" Luna said.

Scarlett, Mags, and Dakota stopped walking and turned around to face her. Mags made a circular motion with her hands as if to say, *Get on with it*.

"My mom may not be a real psychic, but her methods aren't totally off the mark," Luna whispered, careful not to let anyone else hear.

Scarlett and Mags looked at each other, confused, before the answer dawned on them. Luna could tell they knew what she meant.

"I bet she has some extra sage lying around. I'll swipe some from her room when she's on set," Luna said.

Chapter 7

WHO CAN THINK ABOUT RAVIOLI AT A TIME LIKE THIS?

It was lunchtime on Monday, and the carnival was empty. And while Principal Mabry gave them a little leeway with school rules when it came to their arrangement, she probably didn't mean "go to the carnival with no adult supervision during school hours."

They hid behind anything big enough as they dashed from ride to ride until they reached the funhouse at the far end of the carnival. Dakota was the worst of the group at hiding, mostly because she had no idea what hiding meant.

Mags pulled aside the curtain at the entrance and disappeared into the darkness.

"One of these days, we're going to hunt down a ghost that prefers broad daylight," Scarlett said before following Mags into the nearly pitch-black interior of the funhouse.

Once Luna joined, they all turned on their cellphone lights and walked through the maze of glass and mirrors. Dakota followed close behind Scarlett, confused and distracted by all the Dakotas in the mirrors.

"I feel something," Luna said. "It's faint, but I can feel it. Someone's... annoyed? That's a new one."

"That's probably me," Scarlett said. "Today was ravioli day at lunch, and I'm missing it."

"No, I don't think so," Luna said, sounding confused.

"She's joking," Mags said, earning a groan from Luna.

Mags stood aside so that Luna could lead the way and figure out where she felt the ghost's presence the most. But they reached all the way to the end of the maze, and then doubled back, and still nothing—nothing more than a general feeling that something was there.

"This isn't going to work unless we're right in front of the ghost. The way these glass panels are set up will block the flow of the sage's smoke. He needs to be really close. Probably within a few feet," Luna said.

"We're running out of time," Mags said. "We need to find this ghost before lunch is over, or we've wasted another day."

"Wait a minute, I have an idea," Scarlett said. She turned around and faced the mirror behind her and ran her fingertips down the

length of it, her fingers making a high-pitched squeaking sound as they made their way down. In their path was a streak of fingerprints.

She turned to the panel of glass to her right and did they same thing, her fingers making the same high pitched squeak as she did it.

"What are you doing?" Mags asked with a raised eyebrow.

"He used to get angry when kids left fingerprints on the glass. I'm making him angry."

"It's working! I can feel him. He's here. I can't tell where yet, though," Luna said. She rummaged through her jacket pockets and pulled out the bundle of sage and a book of matches, holding one stick at the ready to strike and light the sage.

Mags walked two feet to her left and started slapping her full hand against the glass and mirror panels to leave handprints behind.

"How about now?" Mags asked.

"Mags?" Scarlett whispered. "Mags, come over here please. Don't look behind you, just walk toward me."

Of course Mags looked.

Bill Williams, or at least the ghost of him, glowed faintly behind the glass panel featuring a fresh Mags handprint.

"Oh, good. It worked," she said with a shaky voice.

Luna lit the sage with trembling hands and waved the bundle over her head. She stretched her arm out in front of her as far as it would go without forcing her to move closer to the ghost of Old Man Bill.

Mags grabbed the sage from her, since she was closest to the ghost, and waved it in front of her, with nothing but a glass panel separating her from the ghost.

"You gotta go, Bill. Sorry to break up the party," Mags said.

"This is the worst party I've ever been to," Scarlett whispered.

"Sorry, I don't have anything clever to say. I'm a foot away from a ghost that doesn't like me," Mags said.

The smoke from the sage clouded around them, and they watched as the image of the ghost slowly faded in front of them. Luna breathed in a sigh of relief, having felt like a weight was lifted from her chest.

He was gone. They'd done it.

"You guys," Scarlett said. "Do you know what this means?"

"That we solved another case and that we're the greatest ghost hunters in the universe?" Mags said triumphantly as they dashed from one hiding spot to another on the way back.

"No, there's still fifteen minutes left for lunch. I can have my ravioli and eat it, too."

Mags and Luna rolled their eyes, then dashed off toward the lunchroom.

Scarlett looked down at Dakota, who met her eyes with a wagging tongue and perky ears.

She was very much on board with these ravioli plans.

Instasnap
@PrincipalMabry_01

Ready to get moving on our new and improved science lab! Thanks to all who supported our carnival this year, you know who you are! :)
246 Likes

What is Paranormal Research?

Something that lies outside normal experience or scientific explanation is considered paranormal. When people claim to sense or see ghosts, that is a paranormal experience. Science has not been able to prove the existence of ghosts. On the other hand, there's no conclusive evidence that they don't exist, either.

Paranormal researchers are not necessarily scientists. Scientists have much stricter guidelines for performing experiments that can be tested and retested. Paranormal researchers use the tools available to them to collect evidence, such as electronic voice phenomena (EVP), and electromagnetic field (EMF) readings. They also rely on personal accounts of witnesses who think they are experiencing paranormal activity, and their own experiences in a haunted location. Researching a location's history is also a critical part of paranormal research. An investigator will gather information about the people and events associated with a place to determine if there is a reason for the paranormal activity to occur, such as a sudden death or a traumatic event. Proving the existence of a ghost in a way that can be tested and retested in a scientific manner is quite tricky, since no one's figured out how to catch one yet!

A "Real" Haunted Attraction

The Cedar Point theme park in Ohio is home to some of the biggest roller coasters in the world, but that's not its only claim to fame. It's also home to what many people call the world's only haunted carousel horse.

Daniel C. Muller created Muller's Military Horse in 1917 to be part of a carousel. The ride moved from carnivals to state fairs to small theme parks before ending up at Cedar Point. Daniel's wife loved the horse so much, long after her death, she is said to still visit it after the park closes for the day. Witnesses claim after midnight, the carousel starts up, and Mrs. Muller can be seen riding Muller's Military Horse.

What is a Medium?

In the G.H.O.S.T Squad series, Luna is described as a medium, or sensitive. This means she can tune into the energy of spirits around her, to feel their emotions and communicate with them. Not all people who claim to be psychic are mediums. Some psychics only claim to see into the past and/or future. A medium is defined specifically as someone who claims to communicate with the spirits of people who have passed away. Like ghosts, science hasn't proven these abilities really exist, but they haven't disproven their existence either.

Q&A with Brittany Canasi

Q: Have you ever had a paranormal experience?

A: I think so! When I was younger, my sister and I tried contacting a ghost––any ghost that would talk to us. No one answered, but I was still too scared to sleep alone that night. Early the next morning, just after sunrise, her TV turned on and off rapidly for a few seconds. She swears it wasn't her, and it was happening way quicker than a TV remote could manage.

Q: Would you live in a house if it was haunted?

A: If the ghost was friendly, I could learn to live with it. It could be a pretty cool story for friends! But if the ghost wasn't friendly, I'd try to get rid of it. If that didn't work, and it refused to leave, then I would!

Test Your Reading Comprehension!

1. Why did the principal need the G.H.O.S.T. Squad's help? What was at stake?
2. When Mags and Luna went to the funhouse, what caused the EMF meter to spike at first?
3. Who was the ghost that was haunting the funhouse?
4. How did the G.H.O.S.T. Squad come up with a way to get rid of the ghost?
5. What did the G.H.O.S.T. Squad do to make the ghost appear?

Further Reading

For more information, check out your local library for books on ghost lore. Many books focus on specific regions. You may discover some haunts in your own hometown! You can also look for books on paranormal research and equipment such as electromagnetic field (EMF) detectors. If you're interested in a specific place that's rumored to be haunted, dig into public records and periodicals such as old local newspapers to see what you can find out about the people who once lived or worked there. Is there a mystery to be solved that might explain reports of a haunting? Try to solve it!